Snipp, Snapp, Snurr
and the Big Surprise

Maj Lindman

Albert Whitman & Company
Morton Grove, Illinois

The Snipp, Snapp, Snurr Books
Snipp, Snapp, Snurr and the Buttered Bread
Snipp, Snapp, Snurr and the Gingerbread
Snipp, Snapp, Snurr and the Red Shoes
Snipp, Snapp, Snurr and the Reindeer
Snipp, Snapp, Snurr and the Surprise
Snipp, Snapp, Snurr and the Yellow Sled
Snipp, Snapp, Snurr Learn to Swim

The Flicka, Ricka, Dicka Books
Flicka, Ricka, Dicka and the Big Red Hen
Flicka, Ricka, Dicka and the Little Dog
Flicka, Ricka, Dicka and the New Dotted Dresses
Flicka, Ricka, Dicka and the Strawberries
Flicka, Ricka, Dicka and the Three Kittens
Flicka, Ricka, Dicka and Their New Friend
Flicka, Ricka, Dicka Bake a Cake

Library of Congress Cataloging-in-Publication Data available
from the Library of Congress.

ISBN 0-8075-7490-2
Copyright © 1937, 1996 by Albert Whitman & Company.
Published in 1996 by Albert Whitman & Company,
6340 Oakton Street, Morton Grove, Illinois 60053. Published simultaneously
in Canada by General Publishing, Limited, Toronto. All rights reserved.
No part of this book may be reproduced or transmitted in any form or by any
means, electronic or mechanical, including photocopying, recording,
or by any information storage and retrieval system, without permission
in writing from the publisher.
Printed in the United States of America.
10 9 8 7 6 5 4 3 2

The text is set in Futura and
Bookman Old Style.

Snipp, Snapp, and Snurr went with their mother to say goodbye.

Snipp, Snapp, and Snurr were three little boys who lived in Sweden long ago.

One evening, their father left on a business trip. The next morning, their mother was going on a boat trip to see an old friend.

Snipp, Snapp, and Snurr went with their mother to say goodbye. Snipp and Snapp carried the big suitcase between them. Snurr carried the small bag and held Mother's arm.

Mother hurried aboard, and the three little boys stood on the dock, waving to her as the ship left shore.

"We'll surely miss Mother," said Snurr as they started home. "But I hope she has a good time."

When they got home, they found Nanny stirring cake batter at the kitchen table.

The boys loved Nanny. She would stay with them until Mother and Father returned.

"Good morning, Snipp, Snapp, and Snurr," said Nanny. "How you boys grow! Are you too big to like surprises?"

"No! We will never be too big for surprises," said Snipp.

Nanny laughed. "I had planned this cake... but now you've seen it."

"I have an idea," said Snipp. "Let's plan a big surprise for Mother."

"But what can it be?" asked Snapp.

"Let's get her a chair," said Snurr.

"She'd like that!" said Snipp and Snapp.

They found Nanny stirring cake batter at the kitchen table.

Nanny suggested that they pay for the chair by working for all the people who would help to make it.

"My brother, Anders, makes frames for chairs," she said. "I know there are many errands you can do for him. When the chair is made, you can buy the cloth, and I'll make the cover."

The boys ran to Anders' shop. They took off their caps politely and said, "Good morning! We've come from your sister, Nanny."

Snurr said, "We'd like to get a chair for Mother for a big surprise. Nanny said she'd cover it, but first we need a frame. Will you make it?"

"I will," said Anders.

They took off their caps politely.

B ut I haven't told you everything," said
Snurr. "We want the chair, but we have
no money."

"May we do some work for you while
you make the frame for us? We'll be glad to
do anything," said Snapp.

Anders agreed to let them work for him.
Soon Snipp was sweeping the floor, Snapp
was carrying boards to the bench, and
Snurr was looking for nails the right size for
the chair.

At last, the frame was finished.

"It's straight and strong," said Anders.
"That frame will last for many, many years."

Anders agreed to let them work for him.

There's an old friend of mine, Lars, across the street who is an upholsterer. He knows how to put springs in a chair and stuff it so that it will be soft and comfortable," said Anders. "Why don't you go offer to work for him next?"

The three little boys thanked Anders and carried the sturdy frame into Lars' shop. A smiling man in a long white coat came to meet them. Snipp, Snapp, and Snurr found it easy to tell him about the big surprise.

"I'll put in the very best springs I have, and I'll use the best material to stuff the chair," said Lars. "Then I'll put strong cloth over the stuffing so the chair will be ready for a slipcover."

A smiling man in a long white coat came to meet them.

That's good, but you see, we have no money," explained Snapp. "May we work for you, while you are making the chair for us? We'll be glad to do anything."

"Go into my workroom and make it neat and tidy," said Lars.

The three little boys worked hard. Snipp and Snapp put feathers in bags. They found many pieces of cloth which they folded into neat piles. Snurr swept the floor, and then he carried out sacks full of strings and scraps.

At last, the upholstering was finished. And the workroom was all straightened.

"Sit down in your chair and see how you like it," said Lars.

Snipp sat down and said, "Oh, it is soft!"

Snapp sat down next and said, "It's very comfortable."

The three little boys worked hard.

And Snurr said, "Thank you very, very much. I'm sure Mother will like this the best of any chair she has ever had."

Lars smiled as he said, "I think you are right."

He helped the three boys put the chair on a two-wheeled cart, and they started down the street.

Snipp pulled the cart, Snapp held the chair in place, and Snurr ran behind to be sure the chair didn't fall off.

"Let's stop right here," said Snipp, when they were in front of a small shop. "We'll go in and try to get some pretty cloth to cover the chair."

The boys put the chair on a two-wheeled cart.

The three little boys hurried into the shop. Behind the counter stood a man with black curly hair.

"Good morning," said Snipp. "Will you please show us cloth to cover a chair? The chair is to be a big surprise for our mother. She likes red very much."

"And she likes flowers," added Snapp.

"Have you cloth that has red flowers on it?" asked Snurr.

"That I have," answered the man. he held up a piece for them to see.

"Oh, I like that!" said the three little boys all at once.

"Have you cloth that has red flowers on it?"

That is just what we want, but we have no money," said Snurr. "May we work for you to pay for the cloth? We'll be glad to do anything."

When the man understood about the big surprise, he agreed. he measured the cloth, cut it, and handed the package to Snurr.

"Here you are," he said. "You may take this package home, but hurry back! I'll have some work for you."

The three little boys hurried home with the chair and the package.

But they quickly returned to the shop to work. They folded cloth into neat creases on the bolts and put the bolts on the shelves in straight, even rows.

They folded cloth and put the bolts on the shelves.

When the boys came home late that afternoon, they found Nanny busy with the sewing.

"The cover is all cut out, boys," she said. "I have it nearly basted, too."

"Do you think you can possibly have it all done when Mother gets home?" asked Snipp. "You have only one week more."

"Of course I'll have it done," said Nanny. "You three boys are working hard to earn the chair and this cloth. That's your share. Now I'll do my share."

Every day the next week, the three little boys did chores for Nanny, while Nanny sewed on the cover.

"Of course I'll have it done."

The morning of the day Mother was expected home, Nanny said, "Boys, the cover is finished! Let's put it on."

Ever so carefully, they drew it over the chair and into place.

"Isn't it beautiful!" exclaimed Snipp.

"It does fit well," said Nanny.

"Now we must hurry to the boat to meet Mother," said Snurr.

Mother was very happy to see the three little boys.

On the way home, the boys told her they had a surprise. Mother was very curious, but she had to wait until she got home.

As she stepped into the living room, she cried, "It's a chair! A perfectly beautiful chair!"

"It's a chair! A perfectly beautiful chair!"

Later in the evening, Mother made a fire in the fireplace, and the three boys drew the chair before it. Then Snipp told Mother how Anders had made the frame for the chair, how Lars had upholstered it, and how they themselves had chosen the material for its cover.

"And Nanny sewed the cover for the chair," said Snapp. "We worked hard every day to pay for the work each person did in making the chair."

Snurr added, "Everybody was very glad to help us with the big surprise."

Mother smiled as she said, "I know there are many people I must thank for this big surprise, but my three big boys are the ones I thank most of all."

"My three big boys are the ones I thank most of all."